sleepover Girls

Sleepover Girls is published by Capstone Young Readers
A Capstone Imprint
1710 Roe Crest Drive, North Mankato, Minnesota 56003
www.capstoneyoungreaders.com

Library of Congress Cataloging-in-Publication data is
available on the Library of Congress website.
ISBN: 978-1-62370-261-8 (paperback)
ISBN: 978-1-4965-0541-5 (library binding)
ISBN: 978-1-62370-576-3 (eBook)
ISBN: 978-1-4965-2350-1 (eBook PDF)

Summary: Delaney takes her position as the sixth-grade representative on
her middle school student council seriously, and when she discovers that
her lab partner is being cyberbullied she enlists the help of
the other Sleepover Girls, Maren, Ashley, and Willow, to shed
some light on the problem and expose the bullies.

Designed by Alison Thiele

Illustrated by Paula Franco

Printed in the United States of America in Stevens Point, Wisconsin.
052015   008824WZF15

sleepover Girls

Delaney
vs.
THE
BULLY

by Jen Jones

CAPSTONE YOUNG READERS
a capstone imprint

Maren Melissa Taylor

Maren is what you'd call "personality-plus" —
sassy, bursting with energy, and always ready
with a sharp one-liner. She dreams of becoming
an actress or comedienne one day and moving
to Hollywood to make it big. Not one to fuss
over fashion, you'll often catch Maren wearing a
hoodie over a sports tee and jeans. She is an only
child, so she has adopted her friends as sisters.

Willow Marie Keys

Patient and kind, Willow is a wonderful confidante and friend. (Just ask her twin, Winston!) She is also a budding artist with creativity for miles. She will definitely own her own store one day, selling everything she makes. Growing up in a hippie-esque family, Willow acquired a Bohemian style that perfectly suits her flower child within.

Delaney Ann Brand

Delaney's smart and motivated — and she's
always on the go! Whether she's volunteering
at the animal shelter or helping Maren with her
homework, you can always count on Delaney.
You'll usually spot low-maintenance Delaney in
a ponytail and jeans (and don't forget her special
charm bracelet, with unique charms to symbolize
each one of the Sleepover Girls). She is a great
role model for her younger sister, Gigi.

Ashley Francesca Maggio

Ashley is the baby of a lively Italian family.
Her older siblings (Josie, Roman, Gino, and Matt)
have taught her a lot, including how to get
attention in such a big family, which Ashley has
become a pro at. This fashionista-turned-blogger
is on top of every style trend and shares it with
the world via her blog, Magstar. Vivacious and
mischievous, Ashley is rarely sighted without
her beloved "purse puppy," Coco.

chapter One

"I can see it now: Delaney Brand — a new *brand* of leader," said Ashley, skywriting the words in the air as if on an invisible billboard. It was way after midnight, and we were all a little overtired and extra giddy.

Never one to be outdone, Maren jumped to her feet. "America's number-one *brand* — Delaney!" she said, making a big flourish with her hands for emphasis.

Willow giggled, looking up from the cute braided bracelet she was making for Ashley. "Delaney — a *brand* you can count on!"

Pretty soon we were all one-upping each other with more brand-related slogans for my pretend political campaign. Each slogan and idea was more outrageous than the next. I'd never thought much about my last name until tonight. I was pleasantly surprised by its potential.

"You guys are too much," I said. "If I ever do run for office, I'll be sure to hire you as my marketing team."

Maren reached for a pretzel and flopped onto her polka-dot comforter. "*If*, Laney?" she asked. "Try *when*. We all know it's only a matter of time till you're student council president."

Now that had a dreamy ring to it! I had to admit that she had a point. Ever since we'd gotten to middle school, I'd thrown myself into a bazillion different activities. Student council was my most recent conquest. What could I say? I was a joiner.

"Well, when that happens, I'm going to lobby for early dismissal on Fridays," I joked. "After all, don't they know we've got sleepovers to attend?"

Admittedly, there weren't many people at school who didn't know about our weekly sleepovers. After all, we'd been doing them for what felt like ages. However, the whole tradition actually started in third grade.

It first became a tradition thanks to my mom. She offered to watch Maren on weekends when her mom was jet setting on trips for her job. (Ahh, the fabulous life of a travel magazine editor!) One night, Maren's mom returned the favor, allowing Maren and me to each invite one other person. We invited Ashley and Willow. And that's how the Sleepover Girls (as we so originally nicknamed ourselves) were born! Every Friday night we embarked on yet another overnight adventure. We missed an occasional Friday, but it was very rare.

And here we were at Maren's — the place where it all started! I hugged Maren's fuzzy pillow a little closer just thinking about it.

"Earth to Delaney," yelled Maren, poking me in the arm with a pretzel rod. "Salted caramel ice cream is calling our names." Apparently the other girls had been planning a trip downstairs to raid the refrigerator while I'd been taking a trip down memory lane.

We tiptoed downstairs, trying not to wake Maren's mom. (She was still jet-lagged after a recent trip to Chile.) Luckily, she'd found time to go grocery shopping before our sleepover.

The kitchen was full of tasty treats to satisfy our cravings for midnight munchies. There were even a few souvenir snacks she'd brought back from her travels! Ash eagerly dipped her hand into a bag of beef jerky and thrust it out toward us. "Anyone?"

"I'll pass," Willow said, opting for a scoop of ice cream instead. "I'm doing the no-meat thing, remember?" A big animal lover, she'd recently decided to go vegetarian.

"Totally spaced on that, Wills! Props to you for vegging out," Ash said.

Maren stuck her spoon straight into the carton of ice cream and twirled it around. "I think we'll all be tempted to go veggie after the dissection unit coming up in science," she said. "So gross!"

"Even I think it's gross, and I love science," I said. "It's the one part of science class that I dread. But at least Willow and I can tackle it together!" Thankfully, I had Willow as my lab partner to help me navigate the amazing internal organs of dead animals.

"Oh yeah, I've been meaning to talk to you about that, Delaney," Willow said, nervously reaching for another spoonful of ice cream. "I actually got Mr. Tanner to agree to let me do an independent study instead of the dissection assignments. I just can't go there. I love animals too much. I hope you understand."

"I totally get it," I assured her. "But I'm still bummed. What will I do without my partner in crime?"

Ashley handed me a beef jerky stick in consolation. "Just join me and Sophie! There's already one group of three, so I don't see why Mr. Tanner wouldn't let you," she said.

It was the only class I had with both Ashley and Willow, which — coupled with the fact that I loved science — made it my favorite hour of the school day. (Having Maren in the class would have made it too perfect, but a girl could always dream.) The thought of joining their group made me feel way better. Here's hoping our teacher would allow it!

"Sounds like a plan," I said, eager to change the subject so Willow wouldn't feel bad. "Now who's up for watching a DVD?" We were known to fall asleep in front of the TV watching bad horror movies and cheesy chick flicks.

Maren giggled. "I was hoping someone would ask that. Hold that thought!" she said, running over to the counter and grabbing a tote bag. She pulled a pair of 3-D glasses out and put them on. "May I present to you . . . *Zombie Homecoming Queens* in full three-D action!"

Grabbing the DVD, she started walking zombie-style with her arms outstretched toward Ashley, who promptly shrieked and playfully swatted her away.

"Now that sounds delightfully bad," I said. "Bring on the flesh-eating frenzy."

chapter Two

When I got home the next morning, my plan was to catch up on some sleep. (One of the little-known secrets of the sleepover tradition was the long naps that often followed them.) But when I walked into my house, it was clear my energetic puppy had other plans.

"Frisco!" I exclaimed, trying to calm him down as he tackled me onto the couch and started licking my face relentlessly. I tried to yell Frisco's name again, but I couldn't get it out, thanks to a sudden attack of the giggles.

My dad stood in the doorway, shaking his head with a grin. "Looks like Frisco's ready for his walk," he said. "You got home just in time."

My parents never missed a chance to remind me what I'd signed up for when we adopted Frisco. I'm responsible for pretty much everything when it comes to my cute little pup. And I'm totally fine with it, but after only three hours of sleep it was a little tough.

I groaned and shot a pleading look at my younger sister Gigi, who was curled up on the couch reading. "I'll let you use my flat iron if you walk him just this once," I bribed her, hoping she'd take me up on it. She was forever trying to use my hair care products.

Gigi barely looked up from her magazine. "In case you forgot, you already promised me that last time I walked Frisco for you," she said.

"Now, if you invite me to your next sleepover, then we can chat." She was also forever trying to score an invite to our sleepovers.

"Nice try, Gigi," I said. "Not happening." I avoided my dad's disapproving glance and turned my attention back to Frisco. He put his paw on my arm, staring me down with his deep brown puppy dog eyes. Who could resist that face?

"Okay, okay," I grumbled, reaching for my shoes. "You win, Friskers. But I am not changing out of my pajama pants. That's nonnegotiable."

Once we got outside, the blast of chilly air woke me up a little. I managed to perk up enough to keep up with my boundless pup.

As I was trailing Frisco down one of the neighboring streets, I spotted two familiar faces coming my way — Kate Homan, one of the queen bees of the seventh grade, and Sophie

Hanlon, one of Ashley's new besties. Sophie had moved to Valley View from Los Angeles not too long ago.

The Sleepover Girls got off to a rocky start with her. We thought she was super snobby, and it hadn't helped that it felt like she was stealing Ashley away from us. Luckily, we'd managed to hug out our differences since then. Now she even joined us for our sleepovers every once in a while.

"Hey, Sophie!" I exclaimed as they got closer. "What brings you over to this side of town?" She and her fam lived in the more rural, woodsy area of Valley View. I probably looked like a crazy person with my frazzled sleepover hair and pajama pants. There wasn't much I could do about it now.

"Oh, hey, Delaney," she said. "Kate lives right up the street. We were just getting some fresh air before we head to the mall. There are some killer sales today." I wasn't surprised to hear they were hitting the sales. Much like Ashley, Sophie was a serious fashion fanatic.

"Cool," I told her. "Maybe I should go with you. Clearly my style today could use a little help." I gestured at my thrown-together getup, smiling. Kate just gave me a thin, fake smile.

And just when I thought things couldn't get more awkward, Frisco jumped on Kate. He knocked her oversized red handbag onto the wet grass.

"Seriously?" she said, annoyed. Apparently Kate didn't like dogs all that much. She snatched up her bag, brushed it off, and tugged on Sophie's arm as if to say, "Let's go," but I didn't want to lose a chance to plead my case.

"Wait!" I called as they started to strut down the street. "Soph, Willow's not doing the dissection unit in science. I don't have a partner now. Any chance I could join forces with you and Ashley? I promise I'll be a great partner, and you know what a big science nerd I am."

Sophie grinned. "Sure, the more brainpower, the less work I have to do," she joked. "Plus, I'd hate for you to get stuck with someone like Marcie Miner. She's like a science experiment in herself."

She and Kate looked at each other and giggled. Apparently I wasn't in on the joke? Sure, Marcie could be annoying, but the comment seemed a little mean. Maybe she was just trying to impress Kate.

"Well, as long as I get someone to pair up with, I'll be fine," I said. "But I'd much rather team up with you and Ash."

Frisco chose that particular moment to squat and do his business, and Kate decided she couldn't take being around him anymore. "Gross! Sophie, let's go," she urged, holding her nose dramatically.

"Shopping awaits," she said, quickly turning to follow Kate.

I bent down to clean up after Frisco, watching them walk away. I wasn't sure why Sophie bothered to be so buddy-buddy with Kate. I definitely wouldn't be signing up to become one of Kate's many fangirls any time soon. I was perfectly happy sticking with my sixth-grade slumber party buddies, thank you very much!

One adorable bulldog encounter and another lap around the block later, Frisco and I were finally back home. I eagerly went upstairs to crawl into bed, only to find Gigi camped out in our bedroom with my mom cleaning out her closet. Ugh! I guess beauty rest just wasn't in the cards today.

chapter Three

Luckily, a good night's sleep and the right breakfast worked wonders. The next day at school, I was back to my usual bright-eyed and bushy-tailed self. (Much to the dismay of my locker neighbor Maren, who wasn't quite so awake first thing in the morning.)

"Laney, your locker is totally and completely ridiculous," said Maren, peering into my locker as I grabbed my science book from the shelf. "Could you *be* more organized?" Next to her overflowing, messy locker, mine looked like Martha Stewart had personally designed it.

Willow had helped me line my locker with some cute wallpaper, and I'd put in several shelves for easy access to my books and supplies. Amid various pics of me and my besties, I'd added a dry-erase board for my to-do list and a mini calendar for keeping track of my hectic schedule.

On tap for this week? A looming deadline for the school newspaper, multiple soccer practices, and a student council meeting — along with the dissection unit in science class, which was exactly where I was headed. It was the first time in my life I was dreading science class!

"Good luck, chica," called Maren after me, making me smile. "I'm sure you're in for lots of formaldehyde fun!"

Maren always had a colorful way of making even the most boring or dismal things seem like something to look forward to. It was just one of her many talents.

I managed to make it to class a little early so that I could ask Mr. Tanner about joining Ashley and Sophie's group. I was a little nervous to talk to him. However, I was one of the top students in class and always worked really hard. I hated to feel entitled, but I did feel like I deserved to pick my group.

"Mr. Tanner," I started, clearing my throat. "As you know, Willow is no longer doing the dissection unit in class."

"Since I made that decision, I am aware of it," he said, smiling.

"Well, I was really hoping to join Ashley and Sophie's team. They're totally up for it, and I know we'll make a great trio," I said, flashing Mr. Tanner my best earnest expression.

"I see you have already thought about this. However, since Willow isn't taking part in this portion of class, that gives us an even number of students," he said.

"It does," I said, getting a bad feeling about this and where it was going.

"It makes more sense for me to split up the group of three and pair you with one of the partners. That way you'll be able to get more hands-on experience with our frogs," he said. "I'm sure you wouldn't want to miss out on any of our science fun, would you?"

"I guess you're right," I mumbled, not pleased with the final decision.

Mr. Tanner made some notes in his lesson planner as students started trickling in. His face brightened as Marcie walked into the room.

"Marcie Miner, just who I was looking for!" he said, waving her over to us. "Delaney needs a partner for the dissection unit this week.

Instead of continuing to work with Noelle and Grace, I'm going to have you partner with Ms. Brand."

I managed to summon a fake smile to be polite, but I was kind of irritated. Why couldn't I just have worked with Ashley and Sophie? I felt kind of mean being disappointed, but Sophie and Kate hadn't been totally off in their comments about Marcie.

Marcie was always making really obnoxious comments, and she was one of those people who tried really hard to get noticed — but not always in a good way.

But today, Marcie barely nodded at me and Mr. Tanner. She just kept her head down as she trudged over to our shared workstation. I hugged my books to my chest and walked over to greet her so we could start things off on a good note. I wasn't going to let this little bump in the road ruin my day.

"Hey, Marcie!" I called, but my voice did this weird hiccup thing. I decided to try to make her smile. "Oops, guess I got a *frog* in my throat."

She didn't even look up. She just kept staring at her notebook as if it were the most interesting thing she'd ever seen. I was a great science partner, so I wasn't sure why she seemed so upset. This was going to be a long week.

I snuck a look at Ashley and Sophie, who were laughing happily. I didn't have time to get their attention because Mr. Tanner dimmed the lights so we could watch a video all about the life cycle of frogs.

"Frogs belong to a group of cold-blooded animals called amphibians . . ." began the announcer as a visual of a leaping frog filled the screen.

I was actually kind of caught up in the video (yep, I really was a science nerd) when I felt a hand tap me on the shoulder. I turned around to see Grant Thompson passing me a note. Before I could ask him whom it was from, he crooked his finger and pointed over at Sophie, who was stifling a giggle. I quickly put it on my lap so Mr. Tanner wouldn't notice and opened up the crumpled piece of pink notebook paper:

Sorry you got stuck with Marcie! Wish you were over here with us. But I guess it's kind of fitting that you ended up with a swamp creature! j/k. We'll buy you a smoothie at lunch as a consolation prize. – Soph

I quickly covered the piece of paper with my hand and tucked it into my notebook. I definitely didn't want Marcie to see it! I wasn't sure why Sophie had developed such a grudge against Marcie, but it seemed Marcie had taken up permanent residence on her bad side.

Once Mr. Tanner flicked the lights back on, he had each set of partners work together to fill out a worksheet about how frogs and humans were similar. Ready to work, I opened up my notebook (careful not to open to the part where Sophie's note was) to jot down our thoughts.

"Okay, first question," I said, excited to focus on science again. "How is the anatomy of a frog similar to that of a human?"

I started writing a list of ideas, but Marcie didn't even flinch. She seemed more interested in doodling in her notebook. By the time the bell rang, we were only halfway through the worksheet. I'd been hoping we could bang it out by the end of class so I wouldn't have any science homework.

"I have soccer practice after school," I told Marcie. "Want to get together and finish this up after that? We could meet at the library or something."

Marcie twirled her hair around her finger nervously. "Why don't you just come over to my place? I live close to the practice field. Give me your number, and I'll text you my address. You can let me know what time you're headed my way."

I nodded in agreement. "I'm sure my parents will be cool with that," I said as she headed out of the room.

I had no idea what Marcie's problem was, but I sure hoped her attitude would change.

chapter Four

The lunchroom was already buzzing by the time I made it to the cafeteria. I spotted Ashley and Sophie by the smoothie stand. I rushed over to join them. Sophie's face lit up when she saw me.

"Here!" she said, thrusting a strawberry-banana smoothie into my hand. "Don't say I never kept a promise. Glad you survived an hour with your gross lab partner."

Ashley just rolled her eyes and shrugged, as if to say, "That's Sophie."

I wanted to ask Sophie why she was so anti-Marcie, but before I got the chance, Maren twirled in between us. "Guess who's going to the Bahamas over holiday break?" she said, doing a little happy dance. "This girl!"

Maren was forever accompanying her mom on trips for her travel magazine job. "You are so lucky!" I said. "Be sure to send us some sunshine."

Valley View was known for its wet, icky winters, and this one was shaping up to be no different.

"Yeah, and bring me back some sundresses," begged Ashley, who was forever amping up her already considerable wardrobe. "Those Caribbean sarongs are too cute, and we all know we won't be seeing those in Valley View any time soon."

Maren grinned. "Done deal," she said.

"Come on guys, we can't leave Willow sitting by herself all day," Ashley said, waving across the cafeteria at our friend. "Plus, I'm starving."

We all followed Ashley except for Sophie, who was headed in the opposite direction with her tray. "I'm going to sit with Kate and her group today," she told us. "I'll take a rain check for tomorrow?"

Seemed like Sophie was definitely getting in good with the seventh-grade crowd. I had to wonder how Ashley felt about her new friend drifting away. Personally, I'd have much rather sat with my girls than the mean older girls, but to each her own, I guess.

"Okay, but tomorrow you owe me a smoothie for ditching," joked Ashley. Guess she didn't mind all that much.

Sophie hurried over to Kate's table, where Kate was sitting with her boyfriend, Sam Moore, and a bunch of her other followers. Meanwhile, we joined Willow in our usual corner.

"Laney!" exclaimed Willow as I sat down and started unpacking my paper bag lunch. "How did science go? Are you working with Ashley and Sophie now? I thought of you the whole time I was in the library."

"Things did not go how I was hoping they would," I said.

"Oh, no!" Willow said, truly looking sorry. "What happened?"

"Mr. Tanner put me with Marcie, who's apparently totally checked out. She hardly said a word the whole time! I might as well have been on my own," I said, sighing.

"Marcie isn't usually so quiet, is she?" Willow asked.

"No, which was strange," I said. "She wouldn't even look at me! To make matters worse, we only got half of our worksheet done."

Refusing to let me get depressed, Maren put her arm around me. "Here, I have the perfect thing to cheer you up," she said, pulling out her iPad. "I watched this video on YouTube this morning. I haven't stopped laughing since!"

We all leaned in so we could see the video, which consisted of a golden retriever who kept growling at his own foot. Pretty soon we were all laughing hysterically.

"Maybe I should start a channel for Frisco," I told everyone once we all calmed down.

"Only if Coco can be his co-star," Ashley insisted, referring to her beloved purse-sized puppy. "I don't know why I haven't put any videos of her up on YouTube yet. I feel like all I ever do is post things online! How could I ignore my cute little pup? She could be a huge star by now!"

Ash had her own fashion Tumblr blog called "Magstar." She'd gotten quite a following with her stylish selfies and designer obsession posts. Coco had made plenty of photo cameos on her blog modeling doggie outfits, but maybe she and Frisco did deserve a spotlight all their own.

"What's going on?" asked Willow's twin Winston, plunking down next to Maren and giving one of her red curls a tug.

He and Maren liked to act all coy, but they were definitely crushing on each other. It'd been really funny to watch Maren slowly reverse her grossed-out-by-boys stance over the past few months. Usually, Ashley was the boy-crazy one of the bunch. Luckily, Willow was totally cool with her brother and bestie hanging out.

Maren started the video again so we could show Win, and pretty soon we were all cracking up again. But out of the corner of my eye, I couldn't help but notice Marcie sitting all alone in a corner. I felt bad. Something was definitely going on with Marcie. She usually sat with a big group of people. Where were all her friends? I made a little vow to be extra nice to her during our study session after school. Everyone could use another friend, right?

chapter Five

And that was exactly what I reminded myself when I rang her doorbell later that day. When Marcie answered the door, I raised a bag of snacks my mom and I had picked up on the way over from my soccer practice.

"I come bearing gifts," I said, smiling. "Girls gotta eat!"

"I'm not hungry, but thanks," said Marcie, waving me in. She led me to her bedroom, which was covered with posters of WWE wrestlers and bookshelves full of graphic novels. Looking around, I realized I barely knew Marcie.

"I didn't know you were into manga," I said, picking up one of the books and paging through it.

Marcie seemed to warm up a bit. "Yeah, I actually make my own, too," she said, opening her journal to show me a drawing she'd done. But when I went to take the journal from her to get a closer look, Marcie shut it quickly, placing it back on the desk.

"C'mon, let's get started on our homework," she said.

I wasn't going to argue with that. The sooner we finished, the sooner I could get home and start on the rest of my giant homework pile. I pulled up a chair to her desk and opened my binder to the worksheet we'd only half-completed earlier that day. But once we got started, the snail's pace continued. It felt like pulling teeth to get Marcie to participate.

"Let's take a little break," I urged, reaching for her computer keyboard. "Here, I'll show you this hilarious YouTube video I saw earlier today at lunch."

But Marcie snatched the keyboard away from me before I could type in the web address. "Don't!" she exclaimed, her face turning red. "I don't want anyone else going on my computer."

"Sorry," I said, equally embarrassed and confused.

That was a really odd and dramatic reaction to me touching her computer. What did she have to hide? I decided to just address the elephant in the room and see what was bothering her.

"Okay, I get it," I said, putting my hands up to show I surrendered. "Totally none of my business, but is everything okay? I know we don't know each other well, but you haven't really seemed like yourself today."

Marcie cleared her throat, and it looked like she was holding back tears. "You wouldn't understand," she said, turning away from me.

"Try me," I said. "I am a great listener."

Her face crumpled and the tears that had threatened to spill out did just that. "Fine, what do I have to lose?" she said, looking defeated. "After all, I don't really have any friends left."

I had no idea what Marcie was talking about, but I was really hoping I could help her. She seemed completely depressed.

A defeated Marcie clicked on her computer so I could see what was on the screen. "Someone made a fake Twitter account pretending to be me," she said, shaking her head. The username at the top of the page read "Messy Mi-Nerd" and the caption underneath read, "My name is Marcie Miner, and I just love stealing other people's boyfriends." The picture was a Photoshopped image of her face on a cow.

I gasped, and Marcie started crying even harder. "Keep reading," she said. "It gets worse."

The fake Tweets read things like, "Did you see me picking my nose today during homeroom? Now I know why they call me a gold digger!" and, "Why can't I be one of the skinny girls? Oh, that's right, because I'm a cow. #moo."

My heart sank as I read through all of them. Each statement seemed to be meaner than the last. I wanted to ask her what she thought the "stealing boyfriends" comment meant, but it didn't seem like the right time to bring that up. By this point, Marcie was bawling her eyes out. I gave her a hug, hoping to calm her down.

"This is so not right," I said, my blood boiling. "Who would do this?"

She shook her head sadly. "Oh, that's not all," she said. "I've gotten tons of mean emails, and there are lots of rumors going around school about me. Most of my so-called friends won't even talk to me anymore because my fake Twitter says bad things about them."

"This doesn't even make sense," I said. "Why is this happening?"

"It's all because Kate's boyfriend Sam and I were messaging back and forth for a while about WWE wrestling," Marcie said. "That's all we talked about. Now he won't talk to me, either. So stupid!"

"And Kate thought you were trying to steal her boyfriend?" I asked.

"Apparently," Marcie said, wiping her eyes some more.

Wow, I'd had no clue! Even though I was involved in lots of activities at school, I tended to stay in my safe Sleepover Girls bubble when it came to any drama at school. I was surprised none of the other girls mentioned something to me, but maybe they thought it wasn't any of their business.

The Sleepover Girls tried to stay out of senseless school drama, and I totally agreed. However, if we could help Marcie, then we had to get involved. This was beyond a little teasing. This was ful- out bullying and had to be stopped!

"I think you should tell one of the guidance counselors," I told her. "I'll come with you! This can't go on anymore."

Marcie shook her head violently. "No way!" she said, getting even more flustered. "That would just make things worse. And you better not tell anyone! You promised, remember? You can't say anything to anyone — not even the other Sleepover Girls, got it?"

"Okay, okay," I said, feeling deflated.

I had promised, but I also wanted to help. My mind couldn't help wandering back to my encounter with Kate and Sophie and how mean they'd been about Marcie. It couldn't be them, right? I quickly dismissed the thought. Sophie might have been a little rude sometimes, but her bark was way worse than her bite. No way was she capable of doing something so vicious.

I tossed and turned that night, feeling torn about what I'd learned. My mood didn't improve the next day at school. When someone was in trouble or needed help, my nature was to do something. (How do you think I ended up rescuing Frisco?) It didn't feel right sitting on the fact that Marcie was being bullied, even though I'd promised not to tell anyone.

Not surprisingly, sweet and sensitive Willow immediately picked up on my mood the next morning at school. "Want to talk about it?" she asked as we headed down the hallway to class.

"I wish," I said, rubbing my charm bracelet to make myself feel better. (It had a charm to represent each Sleepover Girl: a paint palette for Willow, a drama mask for Maren, a pair of kissy lips for Ashley, and a dog bone for me.)

"Just feeling a bit tired, I guess. Oh, and now I have to go cut a frog open. So gross!" I wasn't sure if Willow bought my excuse, but at least she pretended.

She patted my back in encouragement. "Here, I have something to cheer you up," she offered, reaching into her backpack. "I made this last night to make up for not being your lab partner."

She handed me a tiny pop-art-style neon painting of Frisco. It looked like one of Andy Warhol's masterpieces (but better because it starred Frisco).

"Just a little something you can hang in your locker," Willow added.

"I couldn't love it more!" I said, managing a smile for the first time that day. "Is there anything you can't do?"

Willow grinned. "Yep. Cut a frog open." She giggled. "Good luck, Laney!" And with that, she was off to the library.

How lucky was I to have such good friends? I couldn't help but think about poor Marcie and her friend problems. True friends would stick by you no matter what.

When I walked into Mr. Tanner's classroom, the strong smell hit me right away. Ugh. Everyone was crowded around the back wall. The trays of preserved frogs were lined up and ready. Grant Thompson had picked a frog up by the legs and was chasing around Ashley and Sophie, who were simultaneously screaming and giggling. (Did I mention that Ash had a crush on Grant?)

"That's enough, Grant," scolded Mr. Tanner. "Put the frog back. Now."

Grant begrudgingly put it back, but not before he made a weird lizard face at Ashley.

Once everyone started going back to their seats, I realized Marcie was nowhere to be seen! Had she skipped school? Turned out Mr. Tanner had the answer to that question.

"Delaney, Marcie's out sick today," he said. "So you'll get to partner with Ashley and Sophie after all."

I tried to hand him our completed worksheet, but he just shook his head. "Keep it for reference." He sighed and rolled his eyes, and I followed his gaze over to Ash and Sophie, who were flirting with Grant again. Typical.

As I walked toward their station, Ashley caught my eye and did a silent clap with her hands to show her excitement. I tried to mirror her enthusiasm, but it was hard. Originally all I'd wanted was to pair up with them, but now I was just worried about Marcie. It seemed my no-drama policy was starting to be a thing of the past!

"Okay, everyone, before we dive in, let's do a quick refresher on lab safety and go over each of the tools we'll be using," started Mr. Tanner as I pulled up a stool to sit with Ashley and Sophie.

As he went through the long introduction, Sophie leaned over to whisper in my ear. "Heard Marcie's sick," she said. "Hope the poor thing doesn't *croak*." Ashley overheard and started giggling, but I stayed stone-faced. What was Sophie's problem? Instead of egging her on, I got right to business.

"Sophie, why don't you record our data on the lab sheet? Ashley and I can be in charge of placing the frog organs on the chart," I said, putting the lab tools neatly in a row. I was ready to get this over with.

"Yes, ma'am!" Ashley said with a salute. She was used to my bossy ways. "But you have to do the first incision. I don't think I can handle it!"

I reluctantly agreed. I put on my gloves and grabbed the frog so I could turn him to be belly up. The smell of formaldehyde almost knocked me over!

"Well, here goes nothing," I said. Sadly, dissecting the frog wasn't the most stressful thing I had going on right now. I couldn't stop thinking about Marcie.

chapter Six

I somehow managed to make it through the rest of the day, but it wasn't easy. All I could think about was finding a way to call Marcie after school to make sure she was okay. As soon as the release bell rang, I sprinted toward my locker so I could catch Maren before she headed to her drama club meeting.

"Mar-Bear!" I exclaimed, out of breath. "I need to borrow your phone. Do you mind?"

She looked a little startled but handed it over. "Sure, Delaney," she said.

I nodded gratefully and headed for the nearest empty classroom so I could call Marcie in private. "Hello?" answered a weak voice on the other end.

"Marcie!" I exclaimed, relieved. "Are you okay? We missed you today in science class. Mr. Tanner said you were out sick."

She was quiet for a few minutes, then broke the silence. "I am sick. I'm sick of being harassed," she said. "Last night, someone posted more Tweets on the fake Twitter account to a bunch of seventh graders saying that I wanted to fight them. I was too afraid to come to school."

Why would anyone do this? I didn't blame Marcie for wanting to avoid school.

"I totally get it," I told her. "Don't you think maybe it's time to tell someone? This is getting out of control. No one deserves to be treated this way!"

Marcie huffed on the other end. "No way! And don't even think about it," she insisted. "I wish I hadn't even said anything. Now you just feel sorry for me. Leave me alone." I heard a click, and that was that.

It was hard to pay attention during my student council meeting. Bullying was wrong, and this situation needed to be fixed. But today I had to stay focused, because it was an all-council meeting with grades six, seven, and eight. And that meant being on my A-game, even as a lowly sixth-grade rep! (Remember, today, sixth-grade rep . . . tomorrow, President Delaney Brand.)

The vice-president, Tyler Mathews, took the floor and made a bunch of boring announcements. Then he called up the current president, Sloane Stevens, for more important business. I loved when Sloane spoke. She was so smart and polished. She was definitely a good role model for my future political domination!

Sloane cleared her throat. "As most of you know, every year we do the Valley View for a Change campaign. We pick an issue that's affecting kids our age to address," said Sloane. "The campaign will take place over the next few weeks, so let's hear your ideas!"

One of the eighth-grade reps raised his hand. "What about video game violence?" he said. "We could examine whether it really is influencing kids in an unhealthy way. I'd be happy to do the research. Can we get a budget to try the new *Grand Theft Auto*?"

Sloane shook her head. "Very funny, Tim," she said, chewing on her pencil. "Anyone have any serious suggestions?"

Seventh-grade rep Samantha, whom I recognized as one of Kate's friends, threw her idea into the ring. "What about a movement to relax the dress code?" she said. "I think it's ridiculous that we're not allowed to wear halter tops and tank tops with spaghetti straps. It's time to transport our dress code out of the Middle Ages!" A few of the girls around her clapped in agreement.

Even though Samantha seemed passionate about the topic, Sloane didn't quite share her enthusiasm. "I hear what you're saying, but it's not quite right for this campaign. Think about something that directly affects Valley View students — something that can help make a real difference in their lives," she urged. Our supervisor, Mr. Squires, nodded in agreement.

Before I could stop myself, my hand shot up. "I know for a fact there are students here at VVMS who have been cyberbullied," I said with conviction, the words spilling out. "Maybe we should do some sort of awareness campaign and ask students to take a stand against this type of behavior."

I saw a few students nodding their heads in agreement, and people were already buzzing with possible ideas to build on mine. But was it my imagination, or was Samantha squirming in her seat a little bit?

"Awesome idea, Delaney!" said Sloane, giving me an approving look. "I think we've found a winner. Hopefully this will encourage anyone who's being cyberbullied to step forward, and anyone who's doing cyberbullying to stop. All in, raise your hands!" It felt great to see everyone raise their hands high in the air.

It was official! Cyberbullying awareness and prevention was going to be our Valley View for a Change project this year. Sloane appointed me one of the point people for the campaign. It felt really good, especially on the heels of the recycling program I'd helped start at school.

I knew this was going to be a great opportunity — not only to keep proving myself with student council, but hopefully to help Marcie and eliminate this problem for good! Plus, I knew just the people to help me make it all happen: the Sleepover Girls.

chapter Seven

And that's exactly what they did at our sleepover Friday! Willow had offered to host since she already had lots of artsy materials we could use to make posters.

"We've got a lot of work to do! Ash, you help Willow gather all the craft materials. I'll help Maren clean up the kitchen from supper." I could feel myself shifting into drill sergeant mode, but I knew I had to or we'd never get anything done. And since this was my idea, I had to make sure it turned out exactly how I'd pictured.

Fifteen minutes later, we were in Willow's cozy living room. Piles of craft supplies and neon pieces of poster board surrounded us. If there was a better place to be inspired, I certainly couldn't picture it.

Willow's parents had placed a glass atrium square in the center of the house, and it had a giant tree growing through it. The back of the living room was all windows, providing an unbelievable 360-degree view of the valley. And right now, the sky was glowing pink, orange, and blue as the sun went down.

"Okay, so the idea is to make signs and put them all over school to promote awareness of the new campaign," I said. "We're also doing a peace pledge party and a giant art installation. It's going to be incredible."

"What is the peace pledge all about?" Maren asked.

"People who want to take the pledge about keeping the peace can trace their hands and sign their names on a big poster. We are going to encourage anyone who signs to make up a creative hashtag about online respect," I explained. "We hope to keep it up all year long as a reminder to all of the students."

"That's incredible!" Maren said, giving me a thumbs-up sign to show her approval.

Willow turned on some music to keep our energy up, and we formed an assembly line to make as many signs as possible. Maren traced the peace sign stencil onto the pieces of poster board. Then Willow cut out the giant peace signs.

Finally, Ashley and I wrote "Keep the Peace! #StoptheCyberbullying" in big bubble letters around the circle of the peace sign.

"So, this was all your idea, right, Laney?" asked Willow as she carefully cut out one of the shapes. "I'm so proud of you. I bet there really are kids who are being cyberbullied at school."

I had to bite my tongue to keep from spilling Marcie's secret. She'd come back to school later in the week, but she'd totally avoided me. Even in science class she'd kept things all business and refused to answer any of my questions about what was going on. I wondered what Marcie would say when we rolled out this campaign. I was hoping she would appreciate all the hard work.

Soon enough, we had about thirty signs made, which was more than enough to hang around the hallways.

Ashley's phone buzzed from her pocket, and she swiftly pulled it out. (Ash's phone was always buzzing with notifications, whether it was people commenting on her blog or "liking" her

Instagram photos. Her phone was practically attached to her hand!)

"Oh, it's a text from Sophie," she said, her fingers flying over the keyboard. "We should have invited her. She would have loved to help."

Again, I had to bite my tongue. I couldn't shake the feeling that Kate was somehow the ringleader of the cyberbullying, so did that make Sophie her accomplice? It was hard holding it all in, but I didn't want to accuse our friend. I also had to keep Marcie's secret.

"Well, we managed to get it done just the four of us," I said, pulling Willow up from the recliner. "Come on, we've been sitting down for the last hour and a half. We need to move! Let's play *Just Dance*!"

"I want to be the red one!" said Maren, doing a little booty shake. "Battle, anyone?"

"It's on!" Ashley said, grabbing my hand. "Me and Delaney versus you and Willow."

Willow swiped the air with her hand to make the song start. Pretty soon, we were all grooving out and trying to mimic the avatars on the screen. It was always hilarious trying to keep up!

When we were done, Winston showed up and decided to get in on the action. "Okay, my turn to throw down," he said, pointing at Maren. "Think you can take me?"

Maren smoothed down her wild curls and smiled. She was never one to turn down a challenge. But before she could show Winston how it was done, Mr. Keys came in from the kitchen. "I think you should battle me," he told Winston. And he was completely serious!

We all started giggling at the thought of Mr. Keys dancing like a pop star. "Sorry to have to embarrass you, Dad, but you asked for it," Winston said. "Willow, pick out a song for us. Be sure it's a good one!"

Ashley whispered something in Willow's ear, and Willow let out a little giggle. "Okay, ladies' choice," she said, turning on an upbeat and undeniably girly Beyoncé tune.

The song started, and we almost died of laughter as Mr. Keys started expertly moving and grooving!

When the scores came up, Mr. Keys had won by a landslide! Winston just covered his face with his hands.

"Out of breath, Winston?" Maren taunted him from the recliner. She high-fived Willow's dad in admiration. "Who's up for round two? I call Mr. Keys on my team!"

chapter Eight

Fast-forward a few weeks, and Valley View Middle School was in full swing with the Keep the Peace campaign. The peace signs we'd made looked awesome all over the halls and in the classrooms.

Today the student council had planned an all-school event in the gymnasium. And as students started trickling into the gym, I felt a little flutter in my stomach.

I'd stationed Ashley and Willow at the pizza table, where they were handing out slices to anyone who volunteered to sign our Peace Pledge. (As far as student council was concerned, a little bribery never hurt anyone.)

We'd created a giant fake computer screen that said "Join the Click" in big letters at the top. Underneath it read, "Join Hands and Take the Peace Pledge to Stop Cyberbullying! Everyone's Doing It!" I had to admit, this was my favorite part of the entire campaign.

"Pledge for peace, and get a piece of pizza!" yelled Ashley in her loudest Italian voice to anyone who passed by. She was doing a great job recruiting! It was so cool to see everyone tracing their hands on the "screen" and making up respect hashtags to write down. Like I'd explained to the girls earlier, our goal was to keep the computer screen in the school entryway all year to remind students of their peace pledge.

I spotted Marcie in the far corner of the crowd, but she just looked away when I tried to catch her eye. Would today inspire her to come forward? I hoped so.

After everyone had eaten pizza and the wall was full of handprints and hashtags, it was time to move on to the next part of the assembly. Maren had mobilized the drama club to perform at the assembly. They were going to act out some cyberbullying scenarios so that people understood exactly what it was and how to recognize it. Ashley, Willow, and I sat together at the front of the bleachers. We were excited to see what Maren and her co-stars had in store.

In the first scenario, the storyline was about a skinny kid named Mario. He feels self-conscious about changing in the boys' locker room. He feels even worse when some kids secretly take his shirtless photo and distribute it online, calling him Real-Life Stick Figure and other mean names. As they went through the skit, I saw a few kids smirk and laugh (especially when everyone was shirtless in the "locker room"). However, most people seemed to be paying attention and absorbing the info.

The next scenarios starred two seventh-grade girls, as well as Maren, Zoey, and Sophie. Now this was going to be interesting. In this sketch, Maren played a new girl in school named Leila. Leila quickly makes friends with all the boys, and the girls get jealous and create a "We Hate Leila" website. The casting was a bit ironic. Zoey was one-half of the "Prickly Pair," a set of twins in our class who had definitely had their share of mean girl moments. And, as for Sophie, I had to wonder whether art was imitating life in this case.

For the final skit, two of the eighth graders acted out a scenario where one boy was bullying another via instant messaging and spreading rumors about him in an online chat room. It seemed like it would have been a pretty good skit . . . until one of the guys completely forgot all of his lines! The awkward silence totally filled the room, until someone in the audience finally yelled, "Cut!"

Embarrassed, the two boys slunk offstage, and Mr. Squires took the microphone instead. "Let's remember that this rally is about respect, both online and off," he said, looking squarely at the heckler.

Luckily, it was time to take the presentation in a more positive direction, and he called me and Sloane onto the stage.

"Did you know that almost half of all kids have been bullied online?" asked Sloane. She confidently made eye contact with everyone in the crowd. She was such a pro. "So if you've been cyberbullied or know someone who has, you're not alone. And this next exercise is designed to show you just that." She handed the microphone over to me, and the butterflies started forming a massive swarm in my stomach.

"Okay, everyone, we're going to do an activity called Take a Walk," I explained. I took a deep breath as all of the homeroom reps helped herd everyone onto one side of the gymnasium. The idea of the exercise was that, as various statements were read aloud, students would walk over to the other side of the room if it was something they'd personally experienced. The hope was that students would realize they weren't alone — no matter what they were going through!

"Take a walk if you've ever felt picked on because of your size, shape, or color," I said, and about one-fifth of the students walked over to the side of the room. I was surprised more people didn't walk on this one.

"Take a walk if you've ever seen rumors being spread about someone online, or had a rumor spread about yourself," I said, thinking about the rumors about Marcie. I watched as she joined the group of students walking across the room. She did it!

Sloane read the next prompt. "Take a walk if you've ever had a photo shared online that you didn't want people to see or seen an inappropriate photo of a classmate," she read, and more students took the walk.

I was up next. "Take a walk if you've ever felt disrespected or misunderstood by another student online," I directed. Another forty or so students headed to the other side. It was very quiet in the gym.

"Take a walk if you've ever seen someone else being bullied online and didn't know what to do," I said. I could definitely relate to the people who walked across the room on this one.

Sloane took another turn. "Last one! Take a walk if you've ever felt alone," she said to the relatively small remaining group of students. Just a handful of people were leftover. No surprise, Kate, her boyfriend Sam Moore, and the rest of their group was left. Apparently they'd never had a problem in their lives.

Kate rolled her eyes and giggled. "Are we done yet?" she asked loudly. "This is starting to feel like that scene in *Mean Girls* where they do the trust falls. Thankfully we don't have to do that. I'd hate to have to catch the fat chick." She looked right at Marcie as she said it.

I couldn't believe it! I decided I'd had enough of her. I couldn't hold it in anymore. "Oh wait, I forgot one," I said loudly. "Take a walk if you've ever been the bully." I exclaimed as Sloane gave me a surprised look.

"In fact, why don't you take a walk and not come back until you're ready to be civil to others? Being a bully isn't cool — no matter who you are!"

It felt like everyone in the auditorium's jaw dropped at once, but I didn't care. It was time someone finally called out Kate.

chapter Nine

That night, my phone was ringing off the hook. People were calling and texting me like crazy. Everyone wanted to talk about the drama that had gone down at the rally. Maren, Willow, and Ashley had pretty much filled up my email inbox and voicemail by this point!

But I was on lockdown in my room. I had more important things to do. My newspaper deadline was the next day, and I was going to write an editorial that no one would forget. This article needed my full attention, so I was definitely ignoring everything else.

My fingers were furiously flying over the keyboard. I was totally lost in thought when I felt a tiny head peer over my shoulder.

"What are you so worked up about?" asked Gigi. "You haven't come out of the bedroom all night. Even you usually take a study break."

I usually didn't talk to Gigi about my problems. However, it might be nice to get her opinion on this situation.

"Gigi, what would you do if you knew someone was being bullied?" I asked.

Gigi didn't even give it a second thought. "I'd do whatever I could to stop the bully in his tracks," she said. "Bullying is wrong and dumb."

"Even if that meant breaking a promise you made?" I asked her. Mr. Squires had done his best to find out why I'd gone off on Kate this afternoon, but I hadn't been able to bring myself to break Marcie's trust. As much as I'd wanted to confide in him and get this thing out in the open, I had made a promise to Marcie. And luckily, I'd gotten off with just a warning about my own behavior.

Gigi looked me in the eye. "I would think about the worst thing that could happen if I didn't tell, and the worst thing that could happen if I did. Then I would compare the two," she said.

Wow, I hadn't thought about it like that. For a fourth grader, Gigi could be pretty deep sometimes. She was right. If no one ever told on Kate, she might drive Marcie to do something really bad. If I did tell, the worst that could happen would be that Marcie would never speak to me again. It could also make the bullying worse, but on the other hand, Kate might back off if she was exposed.

"Good point," I told her. Inspired, I began burying myself in writing again. My article was called "Killing 'Em with #kindness." I had to admit, it was pretty good.

Have you ever heard the saying, "You've got to be cruel to be kind?" While that may sound strange, I've recently realized why it is so true.

Recently, a friend asked me to keep a secret. And telling someone else's secret is cruel, right? But not when the secret is that they're being cyberbullied on every form of social media possible.

On Snapchat, people are writing mean things on top of her photos. On Twitter, someone impersonates her and says things meant to embarrass her and alienate her friends. On email, she gets made fun of and threatened.

All of these things are just plain cruel. And that's exactly why I need to be cruel to be kind — to expose this behavior for what it is.

I was really making progress when my mom yelled up the stairs again. "Delaney, phone call!"

Eye roll — had I not already said I didn't want to talk to anyone? "Mom, I told you no more phone calls," I yelled, irritated. I didn't mean to have an attitude, but enough was enough.

"It's someone named Kate. She says it's important," said Mom, stopping in the doorway. What? I didn't even know Kate knew my name, let alone my phone number. My heartbeat quickened as I took the phone from my mom.

"Hello?" I asked tentatively.

"Delaney, it's Kate Homan," said Kate, sounding annoyed. "I was just wondering if you have some sort of problem with me. Because I'd really like to know why."

If there was ever a time to confront Kate, it was now. As soon as I opened my mouth, a flurry of facts came spilling out — starting from square one with the frog dissection and ending with everything I'd learned about all the bullying Marcie had been through.

"And, all things considered," I said, deciding to just go for it, "all signs point to you being behind the fake Twitter account."

There was a pause on the other end. "Well, you're wrong," Kate said.

I should have known she wouldn't confess. "So you're saying that you weren't upset that Marcie was messaging with Sam?" I asked, not sure where my sudden bravery was coming from. "It seems like more than a coincidence that the Twitter account talks about 'stealing other people's boyfriends.' Not to mention that I feel like every time I see you, you're saying something mean about Marcie."

Kate huffed. "It's no secret that Marcie and I aren't friends," she said. "But if you want to know who created the Twitter, you might want to ask your friend Sophie."

And then she hung up on me.

Was Kate for real? It felt like the bottom had dropped out from under me. If she was telling the truth, that would mean I might have to turn in a friend. Even worse, I realized maybe that person wasn't even a friend to begin with.

chapter Ten

If I was a Twitter topic, let's just say I would have been trending. Between my editorial and my sudden outburst at the rally yesterday, everyone had been talking about me. And I was about to make myself even more notorious, because I was headed straight to the vice-principal's office to tell her everything I knew about Marcie being cyberbullied. Well, everything except who my suspects were.

It wasn't my job to name names with no real proof. I could let the people in charge decide if Sophie, Kate, or someone else was behind it once they reviewed everything. I just hoped Marcie wouldn't hate me forever for telling. But like Gigi had said, the alternative to not saying anything seemed far worse. This was the only choice I could make, even if it meant making Marcie upset. I never thought I'd take advice from Gigi, but I was pretty desperate.

Always a great source of moral support, Willow had offered to sit with me in the waiting room. I hadn't gotten to talk to Ashley yet. I wasn't looking forward to breaking the news that her new bestie was possibly a major bully.

"Laney, have I mentioned that you rock?" asked Willow, putting her arm around me. "Everyone should have an advocate like you."

I fiddled with my charm bracelet nervously.

Compared to this, the frog dissection had been a piece of cake! I'd have much rather done that again than dealt with real-life toads. Who knew so much drama could be stirred up just by switching partners in science class?

"Thanks, Wills," I answered, giving her a little hug back. Just her words were enough to help calm me down a little bit. "And everyone should have a friend like you."

She smiled and nudged her book of crossword puzzles toward me to help pass the time.

A few crossword clues later, the door to Ms. Pryor's office finally opened. I never could have anticipated who would be coming out.

There, walking out of the office, were Marcie and her mom. Marcie's face lit up when she saw me sitting there. Total shocker!

"Delaney!" Marcie exclaimed, rushing toward me. "I need to talk to you. Can we meet up in the hallway after you're done?"

"Actually, why don't you all talk in here?" offered Ms. Pryor, motioning for Marcie and her mom to come back into the office. "I would like to speak with Delaney, too."

I made eye contact with Willow, who nodded in encouragement. I took a deep breath, stood up, and followed them into the office.

Ms. Pryor closed the door as we all sat down. I glanced over at Marcie, who grinned shyly and started doodling on her notebook cover.

"Marcie, why don't you start?" Ms. Pryor said.

Marcie put down her pencil and looked up at me, still smiling. "Delaney, you really inspired me yesterday at the rally," she began. "Your willingness to speak up and confront Kate made me realize that I had to do the same. I told my mom and dad everything, and now we've told Ms. Pryor everything, too."

"I'm so proud of you," I said, lunging at Marcie to give her a giant hug.

Marcie laughed at my dramatic reaction, but she gave me a tight hug back.

I guess that let me off the hook for exposing Marcie's secret. What a relief! Though I'm pretty sure Marcie could guess why I'd been waiting to talk to Ms. Pryor. Luckily, it seemed like we were all on the same page when all was said and done.

"Delaney, your cyberbullying campaign has really helped encourage kids to come forward," said Ms. Pryor. "We made a lot of positive progress yesterday at and after the rally. Thanks to you, we can help Marcie deal with her situation."

Marcie nodded. "I'm not going to stand for being bullied anymore, and I hope no one else will, either," she said. "No one deserves to dread coming to school every day."

I got a little choked up. Not to cheese out, but it felt like the Valley View for a Change campaign really had made a difference! Not too shabby for this little ol' sixth grader. I just hoped that Ms. Pryor could get to the bottom of everything and convince the bullies to back off.

"Thanks," I said. "That means a lot."

But all the warm fuzzies in the world couldn't make what I needed to do next any easier. As I left the vice-principal's office, I knew I still had to confront Sophie, even if just for my own sake. I needed to find out if she was the cyberbullying culprit. The question was how? Should I enlist Ashley to find out? Corner her one-on-one? Invite her to our sleepover tonight?

It turned out I didn't have to make any grand plans. The opportunity presented itself to me after school. I headed into the bathroom, and there was Sophie. She had her makeup bag and its contents spread out on the sink and was applying nude lip liner. She jumped about a mile in the air when I came in, smearing the pencil across her cheek.

"Delaney!" she exclaimed. "You scared me."

I didn't really have it in me to be fake friendly, but luckily, Sophie cut right to the chase. "Kate told me about your conversation last night," she said, coming closer to me and speaking in a low voice. "I hope you're not planning on telling on me."

So she had been the bully. I was more disappointed than relieved to finally find out the truth.

"That's not my job," I told her. "Ms. Pryor already knows about everything and will do her own investigation. It's on you whether you want to do the right thing."

Sophie's face fell as she fiddled with her lip liner. "Delaney, I didn't mean any harm," she pleaded. "Kate was always talking about how upset she was that Marcie was flirting with Sam. One night I created the page to make her laugh. I didn't mean for it to get as out of control as it did. After a while, a bunch of people were posting to the page. It wasn't all me."

"That's really low," I told her. "So you were willing to hurt someone else in order to get in good with the older crowd?" I couldn't believe it. Sophie didn't seem to have any idea how much hurt and harm she'd brought to Marcie.

She sighed and shook her head. "You just don't get it," she said, turning back to the mirror. "Let's talk about it more later. Can I redeem myself by bringing pizza over for your sleepover? I'll get your fave with extra pepperoni."

Pizza, really? It wasn't going to be that easy to win me back. "Sorry, Sophie," I told her. "I'm actually planning on inviting Marcie to join us tonight. I'm pretty sure she'd lose her appetite if you showed up. And I wouldn't blame her."

"That'd be a first," said Sophie under her breath.

For a moment I just stared at her, stunned. Why was she being so mean? Hadn't she learned anything at the rally yesterday? Maybe our original instincts had been right about Sophie after all.

"I honestly can't believe you right now," I said, trying to stay calm. "What is your problem? Wait — I don't really care. If this is the real you, I don't want to have anything to do with you anymore."

Fed up, I stormed out of the bathroom, leaving Sophie with her lip liner and lousy excuses.

I wasn't sure how I was going to share the news about Sophie with the other Sleepover Girls. I knew everyone would be disappointed, especially Ashley. But there was one thing I knew for sure — I had no further interest in being friends with Sophie until she made things right, and that was an easy decision.

The Bully Quiz

Are you a bully, a bystander, or a victim? Add up the points next to your answers and find out!

1. A new girl approaches your lunch table in hopes of sitting down. You:

   a) Explain that this has been your group's special table forever, hoping she'll get the hint. (1)

   b) Let her sit down, but roll your eyes silently at your BFF across the table. (2)

   c) Say, "Sure, the more the merrier!" and ignore the angry looks from your friends. (3)

2. You're dying to know who your pal is crushing on, but only your other friend knows the secret. What do you do?

a) Say nothing. Your pal will reveal her crush when she's ready. (3)

b) Tell your friend that you'll broadcast her crush unless she dishes the dirt. (1)

c) Share a juicy secret of your own in hopes that she'll feel obligated to fess up. (2)

3. You ask a friend to go shopping after school. She says no, but you see her at the mall with another group of girls. What's your reaction?

a) You confront her in front of the other girls. (1)

b) You quickly duck into a store and hope she doesn't see you. (2)

c) You try not to cry when she sees you and ignores you. (3)

4. When a rumor goes around, you tend to:

   a) Believe it. (2)

   b) Hope that it's not about you. (3)

   c) Spread it. (1)

5. It's time for swim team tryouts! You notice some of your teammates covering their mouths and laughing. You quickly realize they're laughing about how one girl looks in her swimsuit. You:

   a) Crack a joke about how skinny that girl is. She looks like a twig! (1)

   b) Grab the nearest towel so they don't get a good look at you. (3)

   c) Can't help but laugh. It's contagious! (2)

6. Birthday sleepover time! Your parents want you to invite all the girls in your class. How do you handle it?

a) You pass out the invites to everyone. However, you make it clear to those outside your circle they're only invited because your parents made you do it. (1)

b) You cringe and wonder if you should tell your mom about the girl in class who has been picking on you. (3)

c) You happen to "lose" a few of the invites. It's not your fault they got lost in the mail, right? (2)

7. What bugs you the most about your friends?

a) When they act weird toward me, and I don't know why. (2)

b) When they get all clique-y and leave me out. (3)

c) When they don't do what I want. I have such good ideas that everyone should just agree with me. (1)

8. You see someone being bullied outside of school. You:

   a) Wonder what the victim did to deserve it. (1)

   b) Keep to yourself. After all, the bully could turn on you if you try to help. (2)

   (c) Be thankful that it's not you. (3)

9. Social media, IMs, texting, all that jazz — to you technology:

   a) Is a fun way to get into mischief now and then. (1)

   b) Is scary. You never know what someone will post about you. (3)

   (c) Lets me keep tabs on what everyone is doing. (2)

10. How do you feel when you and your friends are in a fight?

   a) It hurts my feelings, but I usually give in and say they were right. (3)

   b) Bring it! I'm not afraid of conflict. (1)

c) I try to stay calm and figure out the best way to resolve things. (2)

11. In the yearbook, you're most likely to be voted:

    a) Queen Bee. (1)

    b) Best Personality. (2)

    c) Most Likely to Hide in Her Locker. (3)

12. You and a few others are in competition for the lead role in the school play. One girl pressures you to drop out of the competition. You:

    a) Drop out. It's not worth the hassle, and there will be other plays. (3)

    b) Casually mention to the competition that everyone thinks they would be better as understudies. (2)

    c) Figure all's fair in love and drama club! Whatever it takes to land the role, that's what you'll do. (1)

13. When you get mad, you're most likely to:

a) Use the old silent treatment. (2)

b) Get physical or call people names. (1)

c) Keep it all inside. Getting mad will only get you in trouble. (3)

14. As little kids, you and your neighbor used to hang out all the time. Now she's ignoring you. What do you do?

a) Continue to be nice and say, "Hi." Maybe she'll come around and be friends again. (3)

b) People grow out of friendships all the time. I'll be able to deal. (1)

c) Do whatever she does. Then maybe she'll be my friend again. (2)

14 to 23 points: Bully alert! Time to change your ways.

24 to 22 points: You are a not-so-innocent bystander. It's time to speak up and be heard.

34 to 42 points: You are the bully's target and often the victim. Stand up for yourself! You don't deserve to be bullied.

Note: This text was taken from *How Much Do You Know About Bullying?* by Jen Jones (Capstone Press, 2012).

Can't get enough Sleepover Girls?
Check out the first chapter of

Ashley Goes Viral

chapter One

As the limo neared the red carpet, I could see blinding flashes of light popping all around. Paparazzi and private cars were everywhere. Was this really my life now? And, oh my, was that one of the *Project Runway* judges? I couldn't help but have a moment as I peeked through the window at the glamorous scene unfolding before me.

"Wait, let's do a touch-up before you step out of the car," insisted my makeup artist, Fiona. She was always at the ready with a dab of gloss or puff of powder.

I obediently pouted my lips as she put on one more coat of lipstick to finish off my look. She handed me a mirror so I could check out the total effect — not bad! One of my favorite designers, Sirena Simons, had sent over a handmade party dress designed especially for me, and I absolutely loved it. It was a gorgeous royal purple and had poufy short sleeves and an adorable bubble-style skirt. It was fun, frilly, and fab. If there was ever a dress that fit my personality, this was it!

"Ready?" asked my publicist, leaning over to open the door. I nodded that I was. "You're going to kill it on the carpet!" My dog Coco let out a little bark, as if to say she agreed.

The minute I stepped onto the red carpet, I was swept up into a whirlwind of people, lights, and pure chaos. I loved it! I barely had time to snap a selfie of me and Coco before a little girl sitting in the bleachers screamed and pointed at us. "Ashley! Ashley! Can I have your autograph? Please?"

I whipped out my Sharpie in record time. "Of course!" I said, scrawling my autograph and finishing it with a star. I tried to stand there and talk to my fan, but before I could get a conversation going, my publicist grabbed my arm and ushered me over to the booth of the top entertainment show on TV.

I tried not to get nervous as I stared at the "On-Air" sign flashing above the host's head.

"Ashley Maggio, hi!" the host exclaimed loudly, squinting a little to read her cue cards better. "You're one of the blogosphere's hottest stars right now. What made you decide to start your blog, Magstar?"

I relaxed a little as the host thrust the microphone in my face. After all, I could talk about my blog all day! "Well, I started Magstar a few years ago as a way to further explore my passion for fashion," I replied, looking straight into the camera. "Now it's become practically a full-time job, between my YouTube channel, all the social media stuff, and — of course — the blog!"

The host flashed her mega-watt grin at me. "Well, I'd say that's pretty impressive for anyone, let alone a sixth grader," she said, nodding in approval. "I think you've got a bright future ahead of you, Ms. Maggio."

I smiled right back and put on my designer sunglasses jokingly. "Well, I guess I'd better wear shades, then!" I waved at the camera and stepped back onto the red carpet, where I was greeted with shouts of "Ashley! Ashley! Ashley!" from the crowd in the bleachers. It was truly a pinch-me kind of moment.

The shouts seemed to be getting louder and louder, until it almost felt like they were screaming right in my ear. "ASHLEY! ASHLEY!"

I sat up with a jolt, only to see my three besties leaning over me. Suddenly I was transported off the red carpet and onto my friend Maren's couch. I blinked, struggling to make sense of what was happening. The girls all dissolved into laughter after seeing how out of it I was. "What's going on?" I stammered, trying to get out of my daze.

"Let's just say you fell asleep pretty much right after the opening credits finished rolling," said Delaney, waving the DVD cover in the air. "We've been yelling your name for the last five minutes."

So much for watching a chick flick! Usually I was glued to the screen.

"OMG," I said, laughing right along with them. "I guess that's what I get for staying up until all hours last night updating my profile page for the *Stylish Tween* contest. But it's just such an amazing opportunity!" I was super pumped — our favorite mag was holding a contest to find its "Top Fashion Blogger." The prize? A $500 shopping spree and a chance to be featured on the *Stylish Tween* website with a "Day in the Life" video. Sweet!

Maren grinned. She and the other girls were used to me always doing one crazy thing or another for my blog. "Ahhh, so that's why you turned into Sleeping Beauty," she said. "Now it all makes sense."

I reached for a sip of sparkling water, hoping it would pep me up a bit. Even if winning the contest would be worth it, falling asleep early at a sleepover was really bad form!

"You guys, I had the craziest dream," I told them. "I dreamed that my blog had made me famous and that I was at this fabulous red carpet event dressed in a Sirena Simons original."

Willow giggled and handed me a plate of chocolate-covered pretzels.

"The dream isn't all that far from reality," she said. "I checked out your new YouTube channel the other day, and your videos all had tons of views! My guess is you've got this *Stylish Tween* thing in the bag."

"Oh, please," I told her. "I'm far from the most talented person in this room, let alone on the whole Internet."

And it was true. My BFFs were all totally talented in their own ways. The only thing wilder than Maren's sense of humor was her curly, fire-red hair. I was positive that one day we'd see her name in lights as one of the country's top comediennes. Delaney was the brainiac of the bunch, and she had the straight-A record to show for it. As for Willow, the girl was a true DIY goddess, from crafting to art projects to upcycling furniture. (I was hoping she'd help me make some cool pieces to create a set for my future fashion videos.)

I guess we were all kind of rock stars in our own rights. Maybe that was why we'd been attached at the hip for pretty much as long as I could remember. Our tradition of holding sleepovers every Friday had earned us the nickname the Sleepover Girls at school. I couldn't imagine a weekend without one of our slumber parties.

But I didn't want to take over the whole convo by talking about my blog, so I decided to change the subject. "It's not even midnight yet!" I exclaimed, checking my rose gold watch. "I know what'll get me my second wind — a good, old-fashioned round of karaoke. Who's down?"

Delaney nodded in excitement, but Willow looked iffy. She wasn't exactly the most outgoing person on the planet, even when it was just the four of us. (We were lucky if we got her to play *Just Dance*.) Luckily for her, Maren wasn't feeling the idea either. "Love the idea, but my mom will not be impressed if we wake up the terrible twosome," she said, frowning.

Maren's mom had recently gotten remarried, and her new stepsiblings, Alice and Ace (twins!), stayed with her family every other weekend. It hadn't exactly been the easiest adjustment for Maren to make, but she was coming around slowly but surely. It was all about baby steps, right?

Willow reached into her bag and pulled out her nail art kit. "I've got the second-best thing," she said, dangling a neon pink polish in the air. "Manis for everyone! I brought nail bling."

We were all on board with that idea. After all, Willow was a whiz at nail art (and pretty much every other kind of art, too). As we started getting pretty, I felt my second wind coming on. Being around my friends was just the energy boost this girl needed.

Four BEST FRIENDS plus one weekly tradition equals a whole lot of FUN!

Join in by following Delaney, Maren, Ashley, and Willow's adventures in the Sleepover Girls series. Every Friday, new memories are made as these sixth-grade girls gather together for crafts, fashion, cooking, and of course girl talk! Grab your pillow, settle in, and get to know the Sleepover Girls.

sleepover Girls
Ashley Goes VIRAL
by Jen Jones

sleepover Girls
Delaney vs. THE BULLY
by Jen Jones

sleepover Girls
DOG DAYS for Delaney
by Jen Jones

sleepover Girls
Maren Loves LUKE LEWIS
by Jen Jones

sleepover Girls
Maren's NEW FAMILY
by Jen Jones

sleepover Girls
The NEW Ashley
by Jen Jones

sleepover Girls
Willow's BOY-CRAZY BIRTHDAY
by Jen Jones

sleepover Girls
Willow's SPRING BREAK ADVENTURE
by Jen Jones

Want to throw a sleepover party your friends will never forget?

Let the Sleepover Girls help!
The Sleepover Girls Craft titles
are filled with easy recipes, crafts,
and other how-tos combined with
step-by-step instructions and colorful
photos that will help you throw the best
sleepover party ever! Grab all eight of
the Sleepover Girls Craft titles before
your next party so you can create
unforgettable memories.

Amazing OUTDOOR ART
You Can Make and Share

Awesome RECIPES
You Can Make and Share

Colorful CREATIONS
You Can Make and Share

Fab FASHIONS
You Can Make and Share

Paper PRESENTS
You Can Make and Share

Spa PROJECTS
You Can Make and Share

Super SCIENCE PROJECTS
You Can Make and Share

Unique ACCESSORIES
You Can Make and Share

About the Author:
Jen Jones

Los Angeles-based author and
journalist Jen Jones speaks fluent
tween. She has written more than
seventy books about celebrities,
crafting, cheerleading, fashion, and
just about any other obsession a
girl in middle school could have —
including her popular *Team Cheer!* and
Sleepover Girls series for Capstone.

About the Illustrator:
Paula Franco

Paula was born and raised in Argentina. She studied Illustration, animation, and graphic design at Instituto Superior de Comunicacion Visual in Rosario, Argentina. After graduating, Paula moved to Italy for two years to learn more about illustration. Paula now lives in Argentina and works as a full-time illustrator. Her work is published worldwide. She spends a lot of her free time wandering around bookshops and playing with her rescued dogs.